D1796388

THE HIDING-PLACE

THE HIDING-PLACE

by

ELIZABETH RENIER

Illustrated by Gavin Rowe

HAMISH HAMILTON

LONDON

First published in Great Britain 1987 by
Hamish Hamilton Children's Books
27 Wrights Lane, London W8 5TZ
Copyright © 1987 by Elizabeth Renier
Illustrations copyright © 1987 by Gavin Rowe

British Library Cataloguing in Publication Data
Renier, Elizabeth
    The Hiding-Place.—(Antelope)
    I. Title   II. Rowe, Gavin

ISBN 0-241-12135-3

Filmset in Baskerville by
Katerprint Typesetting Services, Oxford
Printed in Great Britain at the
University Press, Cambridge

Chapter 1

"STAND BACK, STEPHEN! How many times do I have to tell you?"

Stephen moved back quickly, joining the group of mill-workers standing at some distance from the testing-mortar. He recognised the note in his father's voice which meant that if Stephen did not obey at once he could be sent home, missing the excitement of the testing of the gunpowder.

His father had been on edge all day because an inspector had come from Plymouth to check on the powder mills, making sure that the rules laid down for the safety of workers and buildings had been strictly kept. Manufacturing gunpowder was dangerous work. There had been several explosions at the mills, injuring workers, damaging buildings. That was before Stephen's father became manager. Since then, there had not been a single accident and Tom Webber intended there never would be while he was in charge.

The mill-owner, old Colonel Tranton, who had lost an arm while serving in Queen Victoria's army in India, had sited the mills not far from his home on Dartmoor, in open country miles from a town. He said he had started them to create employment in a part of Devonshire where jobs were scarce, but Stephen's father believed it was also to bring some excitement into his own life. The gunpowder was used mainly by the local quarries and the old man liked to go along when blasting was taking place. He never missed the testing of the powder at the mills. It was carried out by firing an iron ball from a mortar, which reminded him of his soldiering days, and always with him was Sampson, an ex-soldier who had been his servant in India.

As the foreman checked the fuse,

Stephen put his fingers in his ears. Ned Yeo touched a match to the fuse. There was a loud bang. The ball was hurled from the mouth of the mortar and crashed into the heather at the foot of the hill which rose above the mills.

"That was a beauty!" exclaimed the mill-worker beside Stephen.

The foreman checked the distance the ball had been hurled.

"The best ever!" he shouted triumph-

antly, and the mill-workers cheered.

All except one, Stephen noticed. Jed Upcott, an odd-job man who helped load the barrels of gunpowder on to the wagons which took them to the quarries, had turned away, muttering to himself. Stephen was near enough to catch some of his words.

"Wish it had blown up the lot of 'em . . . stealing my land . . . I'll get my own back . . . They'll see."

He slouched off, keeping apart from the cheerful band of workers making their way back to the mill buildings.

Colonel Tranton and the Inspector joined Stephen's father. They would be going to the manager's house for some ale and a slice of Mrs Webber's rabbit pie. If Stephen had gone, too, he would have been asked to look after his baby sister while his mother attended to the visitors. He quite enjoyed looking after Bessie now that she could toddle and ride on his back but today he wanted to see his friend, Sam. The son of a moorland farmer, Sam was eleven, the same age as Stephen. He would probably be up near Cuckoo Tor, checking the sheep.

Stephen set off up the hillside, following a rough track which wound between clumps of purple heather and yellow

6

gorse. Soon he was high above the powder mills, looking down on the tall chimneys which carried away sparks and fumes from the stone-built, timber-roofed buildings where charcoal, saltpetre and sulphur were ground down, then mixed together for hours to make the finished explosive. Nearer the road were stables and wagon-sheds and, at a little distance from the mills, the manager's and foreman's houses. He could hear the thud and creak of the huge wheels which turned the water from the moorland stream into power for the machinery and see men and horses going about their work.

Soon he would be in a different world. The track he was following led to The Saddle, a level stretch of ground between two tors. The granite rocks of the tors were awesome even in sunlight, menacing when clouds darkened them. On the far side of The Saddle was a vast area of wild moorland—no buildings, often no human beings in sight, only sheep and wild ponies. In still weather, it was a place of silence so deep that a sudden breeze rustling the dry grasses could make Stephen jump.

Sam laughed at Stephen's awe of the wild moorland. "What are you afraid of — ghosties?" he would ask teasingly.

Sam's family had farmed on the moor for generations. He knew its real dangers — getting caught in a sudden snowstorm, or wandering into a bog or, just below Cuckoo Tor, falling into a deep shaft amongst the abandoned tin mines. And he nearly always had his dog, Shep, to keep him company.

Shep was with Sam now, Stephen saw as he reached The Saddle. They were herding a flock of sheep. Stephen shouted and waved, then scrambled down the hillside to join his friend.

"I'm glad you've come," said Sam. "I've found a ewe on her back and with her wool still on she's too heavy for me to lift on my own."

The boys set the ewe on her feet. She ran off to join the rest of the flock, bleating loudly.

"Silly old thing," said Sam. "I dare

say she was frightened by the blast just now. It scattered the ponies, too. A fine old rumpus your father causes with his gunpowder."

"It was a good test today, the best ever, the foreman said. Sam, d'you know a man called Jed Upcott?"

"Course I do. Everyone for miles around knows *him*. Folks were surprised your father took him on at the mills, knowing what dangerous work it is."

"Father didn't want to," said Stephen, "but Jed said Colonel Tranton had stolen his land and left him to starve, so the colonel thought he ought to offer him employment."

Sam looked scornful. "He only ran a few mangy cattle on that piece of land where the mills are now. I reckon he got his living in other ways."

"How?"

"Poaching, for one." Sam's usually cheery face was serious as he said, "Your father should keep an eye on him, Stephen. He's a wrong 'un. I should've thought the colonel would have known that, him being used to dealing with men."

"Father says Colonel Tranton is too kind-hearted for his own good at times." Stephen pulled from his pocket a big slice of rabbit pie which he had taken from the larder earlier that morning. "Would you like a piece, or have you got your own dinner?"

Sam grinned. "I ate it long since. I'm hungry again now."

They sat companionably munching while Shep watched over the sheep. Then Sam stood up.

"I'd best be moving or Father'll be upalong to see if I've lost his precious flock. See you tomorrow?"

"Not tomorrow. I've got to go to Parson Bradley for a reading lesson."

"Reading lesson," said Sam scornfully. "What do you want with that old nonsense?"

"So I can be manager of the mills one day, like my father, while you're still heaving silly old sheep on to their legs."

That led to a light-hearted fight which they both enjoyed. Afterwards, they went their separate ways. On the crest of The Saddle Stephen turned to wave. "Good old Sam," he said to himself. "I'm glad he's my friend."

When Stephen reached home his father, who was taking the afternoon off, sent him with a message to Ned Yeo, the foreman.

"Remember to change into your slippers," he added.

It was one of the most important rules, that nobody must enter the mills wearing their nail-studded boots. At the gate each man changed into hand-sewn "powder-shoes".

Stephen was passing one of the mixing-sheds when he smelled smoke. *Tobacco smoke*. But smoking was not allowed at the mills, it was far too dangerous. Stephen wondered if he should go back and tell the foreman. Or ought he to make sure first if somebody really was smoking, hidden behind the high stone building?

He walked quietly along the side of

the building and looked cautiously round the corner. He *was* right. Half-hidden beneath an alder tree was a man smoking a clay pipe.

Stephen drew in his breath, then clapped a hand over his mouth but he was too late. The man had heard him. Clumsily, on hands and knees, he crawled from under the tree, and ran.

Stephen was about to run, too, to tell the foreman, when he saw that in his haste the man had dropped the pipe. It lay on the ground, a wisp of smoke still rising from the bowl. It needed only one spark to set fire to any powder dust which might be lying around . . .

Stephen pulled off his cap, grabbed the pipe and rolled it inside, then ran to the stream and flung it in. The dangerous bundle was carried swiftly away on the turbulent water.

"You're sure it was Jed Upcott?" his father asked when Stephen told him what had happened. "You said he was half-hidden under a tree."

"There was a scar on his hand, the one holding the pipe, like the scar on Jed Upcott's hand. And he tore his coat on a branch as he ran away. You could check by that."

"Good enough." His father put a hand on Stephen's shoulder. "You did well, son, acting so promptly."

Feeling very proud, Stephen asked, "What will you do, Father?"

Tom Webber looked thoughtful.

"I'm not sure. It will be your word against his and I don't want you involved. He's a nasty-tempered man, Jed Upcott. I'd not have taken him on if Colonel Tranton hadn't insisted. I've no cause to dismiss him on account of bad workmanship. He loads barrels on to the wagons as well as any other man on the job. But a man with a grudge against his employer, as Jed has against the colonel . . . "

"I think you should dismiss him at once," said Stephen's mother.

"Then he'd have a further grievance. I'll call the men together tomorrow and emphasise the importance of not relaxing any of the safety rules just because the Inspector won't be around again for a while. And I'll have a word with Ned, tell him to keep a special watch on Jed Upcott."

The next afternoon Stephen went for his lesson with the parson. The parsonage was three miles away and usually Stephen rode Tessa, his father's moorland pony, but she had gone slightly lame so Stephen set out early to walk. On his return journey he met groups of mill-workers, trudging home across the moor. One of them greeted him cheerfully.

"Shanks's mare for you today, then, Master Stephen. Reckon you'm not so used to walking as us."

"I don't mind walking," said Stephen, "but this satchel's heavy."

They went on their way and Stephen was alone again, taking a short cut along a narrow track between head-high bracken.

Suddenly his way was barred. Jed Upcott loomed over him, a half-empty bottle in his hand.

"I want a word with 'ee, *Master* Stephen," he said, making a grab at Stephen as he tried to back away. "'Twas you, weren't it, as saw me smoking and told on me?"

Stephen tried to free himself but Jed's hold was too fierce. He smelt strongly of ale.

"Doan't 'ee ever do that again, boy, or 'twill be the worse for you," he threatened.

Stephen swung his satchel, hitting Jed on his shin. Taken by surprise, Jed loosed his hold and staggered back.

"And don't *you* ever smoke at the mills again or it will be the worse for you," Stephen retorted, then ran down the track towards the road, and the longer way home.

He burst into the house, eager to tell his father about Jed Upcott's threat.

But in the kitchen his mother was sitting before the fire, rocking his sister Bessie in her arms, while his father knelt beside her, looking worried.

"What's happened?" asked Stephen.

"Bessie's been taken ill," answered his mother, without looking up. "And you should have been home long since, to ride for the doctor."

"But I couldn't, Mother," Stephen protested. "Tessa's lame. I had to walk."

"I don't want to hear excuses," said his mother unreasonably. "You're never here when you're wanted."

"Just because I went to see Sam yesterday . . . " Stephen broke off as his father gave him a warning look.

"Your mother's very worried," he said. "Ned's ridden for the doctor, on one of the wagon horses."

Then Stephen knew that Bessie's illness *must* be serious. Nobody sent for a doctor, who had to come from miles away and would have to be paid, unless they were very ill. He knew, too, that he could not add to his parents' anxiety by telling them of Jed's threat. And, after all, it *was* only a threat. He had come to no harm. All he had to do was keep out of Jed Upcott's way.

Chapter 2

DURING THE NEXT few days Stephen was kept busy, carrying out his apprentice work at the mills and helping his mother. Or trying to help her, for he seemed always to be doing the wrong thing and getting in her way. Even when he tried reading to Bessie or playing with a hand puppet to amuse her, he was scolded.

"She must be kept very quiet," his mother said. "Doctor ordered that."

At the mills, his father was equally

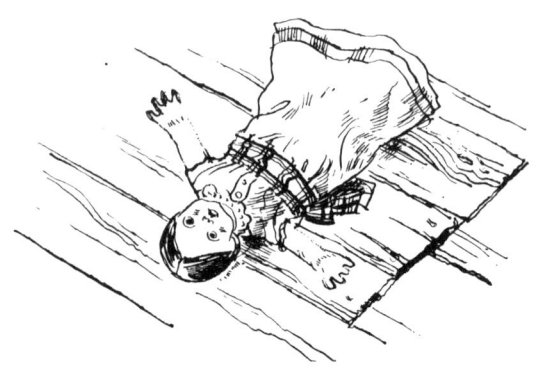

short-tempered. Although the men knew how worried he was about his sick child, some of them found it hard to accept the manager's continual fault-finding. Among these was Jed Upcott.

One morning Stephen came upon him, talking to two other men, beside the wagons they were loading with bar-rels of gunpowder ready for delivery to a local quarry. Their faces were surly. Jed lifted a barrel off the wagon and stood it beside the storage shed.

"Looks as if this one might split," he said loudly. "Dangerous, that'd be.

And with young Master Stephen around, I reckon I'd be blamed instead of the cooper that made it, if there was an accident."

Stephen walked past quickly, feeling Jed's animosity like a heavy hand between his shoulder-blades.

In the afternoon he went to the parsonage for a writing lesson, riding Tessa who had recovered from her lameness. When the parson heard of Bessie's illness he gave Stephen some chicken broth and jelly for her and sent him home early.

"For I've no doubt your mother has need of you," he said, kindly.

But when Stephen reached home he found his mother fast asleep in the rocking-chair and when he tiptoed upstairs he saw that his little sister, also, was sleeping soundly. He felt free

to go up the hill in the hope of meeting
Sam, wanting to tell him about his
encounter with Jed Upcott.

He saw Shep first, on The Saddle.
The dog came running to greet him.

Sam pounced on Stephen from behind a
boulder. In a mock fight they rolled
together into a grassy hollow beneath
the lower rocks of Cuckoo Tor.

Then Stephen said, "Listen, Sam,
I've something to tell you," and Sam's

face became serious as he heard how Stephen had come upon Jed smoking at the mills and how Jed had grabbed Stephen and threatened him on his way home from the parsonage.

"I think you're right to try and keep out of his way," said Sam. "My father was at the inn a couple of evenings ago. He said Jed was there, very drunk and ranting against Colonel Tranton. Going on about having his revenge for the land he was robbed of."

"That's what he was muttering after the mortar test."

"But he couldn't be robbed of the land, Stephen. It belongs to the Duchy of Cornwall, like my father's farm. I expect Jed was behind with the rent and Colonel Tranton took over the lease. Nobody believes Jed's story anyway."

"That probably makes him even more bad-tempered. But I don't see what harm he can do to the colonel. Sampson goes everywhere with him, armed with a rifle. Not at the mills, of course, but Jed wouldn't dare to attack him there. And Colonel Tranton has two fierce dogs to guard his house."

"That's what you should have," said Sam, who could never be serious for long. "Or I'll lend you Shep. You'd give Jed Upcott a sharp nip, wouldn't you, boy?"

But the sheepdog's attention was not on Sam. Shep was crouched in the bracken at the top of the slope, intently watching something below.

"What have you seen?" said Sam, wriggling up to join his dog.

Then he beckoned to Stephen. "Come up quietly."

Stephen crawled up to lie beside Sam. "What is it?" he whispered.

"There's a man down there, creeping along the side of the hill as if he doesn't want to be seen. He's carrying something on his shoulder but I wasn't quick enough to see what it was before he disappeared amongst the alder trees. He'll come out again in a minute. There, look."

The next moment they said together, "Jed Upcott."

And Stephen added, in dismay, "It's a barrel of gunpowder he's carrying."

The boys looked at one another, silenced by what they had seen.

Then Stephen said, "He must have stolen it though I don't know how it would be possible. There's always a watchman on the gate. Sam, what can we do?"

"Find out where he's taking it," said Sam practically. "Or, rather, I can. I know all the moorland tracks hereabouts and can follow him without being seen. Wait here until I get back. You too, Shep. Stay, boy, good dog."

Sam moved off so stealthily that soon Stephen could detect only a ripple in the bracken, no more than a pony or sheep would have made.

It seemed a long time, waiting. Stephen was glad of the dog, alert and watchful, beside him. At last Sam returned, openly now, slithering down into the hollow, breathless and excited.

"He's hidden the barrel! On the other side of the tor, in one of the shafts left by the tin-miners. I can find the place again easily, it's near a stunted alder tree."

"He didn't see you?" Stephen asked anxiously.

"No. I took good care of that."

"Which way has he gone now?"

"Towards the road. He took the track that goes past Colonel Tranton's house."

"But that's not his way home. And, anyway, why isn't he still at the mills? It's not knocking-off time, you can see the men still at work down there."

"*I know*," exclaimed Sam with relish. "He's hatching a gunpowder plot. We must make plans to foil him. We'll . . . "

"We can't do anything, Sam, not until I've told my father. Gunpowder is much too dangerous to leave lying around."

"Exciting, isn't it? What will happen when you tell your father?"

"I expect he'll come and try to get the

barrel back straight away. He'll need your help to find it, though."

"Right," said Sam, eagerly. "I'll wait here until you come." He turned his head, sniffing the air. "I think the weather will break soon." He climbed on to a nearby boulder. "Yes, I'm right. There's a mist coming up. If it gets really thick I'll not be able to show your father the place. It would be too risky to venture in among the old mine workings in a real Dartmoor mist. *So hurry*!"

Stephen ran down the hill, scrambled over the dry-stone boundary wall and raced for the entrance to the mills.

At the gate, the watchman barred his way.

"Whatever be you thinking about, Master Stephen, going into the mills with your nailed boots on?"

"Oh, I forgot," gasped Stephen. He

began to unlace his boots. "I must find my father. Do you know where he is?"

"Over at your home. Doctor's there. You'm in a mighty hurry, lad."

"I've something important to tell Father."

Stephen was about to hurry away when the watchman caught his arm. "Bide a minute. By your face, 'tis bad news you have for him. If so, you'd best be sure it can't wait. He's had trouble enough already today."

Stephen felt suddenly cold. "You said the doctor's come. Is Bessie . . . Is she worse?"

"Not that I know of. 'Tis what happened here at the mills a while back that's upset him."

"*What* happened, Will?" As the watchman remained silent, Stephen asked, "Was it to do with Jed Upcott?"

The watchman shrugged. "I reckon you'll hear about it soon enough so I may as well tell 'ee. Yes, 'twere Jed that started it."

"Started what?"

"A fight. The man checking the wagons said there was a barrel short. Jed swore he'd counted them and 'twas a full load."

"But he took one off. I saw him. He said it was faulty."

"He swore he'd replaced it. So they called the foreman and *he* wanted to know where the faulty barrel was. It couldn't be found. Then Jed accused

39

another man of hiding it, to get Jed into trouble. Then — well, you know, lad, men's tempers are a bit short these days, with your father always seeming to be looking for faults. I'm not blaming him, mind, I know how worried he's been about your little sister . . . "

"So what happened?" Stephen prompted.

"There was a fight. Ned Yeo tried to calm things down but Jed was fighting mad by now, and going on about the mill-owner stealing his land. And when your father arrived, Jed punched him."

"Jed Upcott *hit my father*?" Stephen's voice rose. "That was stupid."

"Jed found that out mighty quick, I can tell 'ee. Your father told Jed he'd been a trouble-maker ever since he came and was a danger to the mills and everyone working here. Ordered him to

pick up his pay and leave at once, and not come back. And Jed left in such a hurry he left his boots behind, they'm in my shed here. So now you see why I warned 'ee to have a care what you say to your father."

"Yes. Thanks. Was the missing barrel found, Will?"

The watchman scratched his head. "Blessed if I know. I reckon all the rantumscour put it out of everyone's head. 'Twill have to be checked, though."

When it is, thought Stephen, it will still be missing. And only Sam and I know where to find it.

The doctor was just leaving. Both Stephen's parents were waving him goodbye and they were smiling happily.

"Such good news, Stephen," his mother greeted him. "Bessie is out of danger."

"Oh, that *is* good," said Stephen thankfully. He waited until his mother had gone into the house, then turned to his father. "I've something to tell you."

"Not now, boy. I must get back to work, and with a lighter heart, thank God."

"It's important," Stephen insisted. "It's about Jed Upcott."

His father turned to face Stephen. "What about him?"

When he heard what Stephen and Sam had seen, he exclaimed angrily, "The irresponsible fool! We must get that barrel back at once. He must have made up the story about it being faulty, meaning to steal it at the first opportunity. Though how he got it out of the mills . . . But that must wait. You said Sam . . . "

Tom Webber broke off as he looked up the hill. The mist had thickened, blotting out the tors and The Saddle, shrouding the trees in the valley.

"Sam will have gone," said Stephen. "He said it would be too risky to venture amongst the mine workings in a thick mist."

His father frowned, then shrugged his shoulders. "It will have to wait until tomorrow, then. Don't look so worried. If *we're* stopped from collecting the barrel, so will Jed be. Go in and get some tea now, then take Tessa and ride round by the road and ask Sam to meet us on Cuckoo Tor at first light. And, Stephen, don't tell your mother about this. She'll only fret and she's had enough worry over Bessie lately. Tell her — oh, tell her I'm sending you with a message to Colonel Tranton."

"That's the way Jed was heading," Stephen remembered. "Father, don't you think it's the colonel he means to harm? He's always going on about the mill-owner stealing his land . . . "

"You're right, son. If Jed had meant to harm me, or the mills, he's had plenty of chances. But to steal that barrel and take it so far away . . . I'll write a note to Colonel Tranton, warning him to be on his guard. You can drop it in on your way to Sam's."

Stephen was thankful now that he had not told his father of his encounter with Jed on the way back from the parsonage. If his father *had* known about that, Stephen felt sure he would not have let him go, especially if there was a chance that Jed was still in the vicinity of the mill-owner's house.

His mother, now that Bessie was over

the worst of her illness, had time to fuss over Stephen.

"I don't like him going," she said as his father was writing the note, "not with a mist coming down."

"He'll keep to the road, Mary, and Tessa can find her way home in any sort of weather. You don't mind going, son, do you?"

"Of course not," Stephen answered confidently enough, then added Sam's teasing question, "What is there to be afraid of — ghosties?"

All the same, as he set out along the high road, his father's note to Colonel Tranton in his pocket, he wished Sam was with him. The air was damp and cold. Drops of moisture clung to the leaves of the stunted trees. Once beyond the clattering of the water-wheels it was very quiet and Stephen

47

was glad of the rhythmic clip-clop of Tessa's hooves. He watched the verge, looking for the two white-painted stones marking the drive which led to the mill-owner's house. He had been there before, invited to the Christmas parties given by the colonel and his wife for the mill-workers' children. The house was

at the end of a long avenue of fir trees,
part of a big plantation. It was always
dark under the trees, a creepy place
even when the sun was shining.

Tessa seemed nervous. She shied as a small animal ran across the road.

"It's only a rabbit, stupid. Hold back, now, this is where we turn in."

The pony obeyed Stephen but her ears were twitching as she started up the drive.

"There's nothing to be afraid of," Stephen said, as much to reassure himself as the pony.

With the mist swirling about them, changing them into strange shapes, the dark trees seemed to be pressing in on him, reaching out to touch him. Tessa stopped in her tracks, trembling and sweating.

Suddenly, from the direction of the house, came the excited barking of the colonel's dogs. A man's voice called, "Who's there?"

Stephen shouted his name but he

doubted if he would be heard above the barking of the dogs. Despite all his efforts, Tessa would not move. Stephen dismounted and tried to lead her.

The dogs quietened. Another voice called, Colonel Tranton's this time.

"What is it, Sampson?"

"Someone about, sir. At least, the dogs think so. And I thought I heard a horse."

"Probably one of the wild ponies off the moor. Fire off a couple of shots, though. If it's poachers, that should scare 'em."

Stephen shouted again. This time his voice was drowned by the sound of the gunfire. Tessa threw up her head, snatched at the reins. She reared, knocking Stephen over, and bolted down the drive, out of sight immediately amongst the trees.

"Just a pony," came the colonel's voice.

"It seems so, sir. All the same, I'll take a look around."

Stephen started to run towards the house. A figure came lurching towards him. Not Sampson. Not the colonel. *Jed Upcott.*

As Stephen gasped the name, he was seized, a hand clamped over his mouth. Then, kicking and struggling, he was dragged into the trees.

"Doan't 'ee dare make a sound," warned Jed. He pulled a rag from his pocket, forced it into Stephen's mouth and gagged him. "Come on, now, before the dogs find us."

The dogs were barking again, coming closer. Stephen struggled to free himself but Jed's grip was too strong as he half-dragged him through the plantation. They came to a low dry-stone wall. Jed hauled him over, then crouched on the far side, listening. The barking, and Sampson's voice, shouting orders to the dogs, were fainter now.

"Good," Jed grunted, " they've lost us. So now, what be *you* doing here *Master* Stephen? Did your father send you?"

Stephen nodded, desperately trying to think up some story that would sound convincing. Jed started to untie the gag. As he did so, he saw the note protruding from Stephen's pocket. He pulled it out, ripped open the envelope, then swore as he tried to decipher Tom Webber's handwriting.

"'Tis beyond me," he said furiously. "What's it say?"

Stephen's mouth was just free of the gag when Jed jabbed a finger on the note. "I can read those words. That's my name. So what be your father writing about me, eh?"

"It's too dark to see," said Stephen, playing for time as he heard the dogs coming their way again.

Jed heard them, too. He stuffed the note into his pocket, replaced the gag. Then, before Stephen realised his intention, Jed hoisted him over his shoulder and ran.

Stephen's head joggled against his captor's back as Jed ran across a rough piece of ground and on to the road. He remembered that Jed was wearing his powder shoes so there would be no sound of nailed boots. Soon he left the road and they were going uphill. The mist was all around them, like a cold grey curtain shutting them off from the rest of the world. Stephen kicked at his captor's chest, pummelled his back with clenched fists. But it was useless. Jed took no more notice than if he had been carrying a baby over his shoulder.

After a while he slowed down and picked his way more carefully. At one point the ground seemed to give way and Jed stepped back, swearing. And then Stephen knew where they were. At the old mine workings! In amongst the abandoned shafts and tunnels, their entrances hidden by heather and gorse, a place where not even Sam, who knew every inch of the moor for miles around, would venture in a mist.

At last Jed stopped, dropping Stephen on the ground. As if by magic, he produced a rope and bound Stephen's hands and feet. Then, as if he were handling a bundle of sticks, he thrust him into a narrow tunnel running back into the hillside. It was dark in there, smelling of earth and fox. And something else. A smell Stephen recognised at once. Seasoned wood. And to confirm his suspicion, something hard was pressing against his side.

"The barrel." He said it aloud, the words strangled by the gag. "The barrel of gunpowder."

"That's right," said Jed, guessing what Stephen had said. "One little spark, that be all that's needed. When

they come to look for 'ee, you'll be blown sky-high. A fine big bang there'll be, heard for miles." Jed laughed to himself. "'Tis your own fault, *Master* Stephen, coming along just as I was spying out the land, planning where to run the fuses. Going to blow up the mill-owner's house I was, and have my revenge on him for stealing my land. That'll have to wait, though."

Stephen heard a cork being withdrawn from a bottle, then noisy drinking. Jed's voice became thicker, his words slurred.

"You shouldn't meddle, *Master* Stephen. Remember that." He laughed again, a long cackle of laughter which made the sweat break out on Stephen's body. "But then you won't be around much longer to *do* any meddling." Jed drank some more, then lay down across the tunnel entrance, blocking it completely.

Soon came the sound of Jed's heavy snores. And Stephen lay in the dark tunnel, bound and gagged, with the edge of the barrel digging into his side, and knew there was no hope of escape.

Chapter 3

STEPHEN LAY ABSOLUTELY still, afraid to make the slightest move in case he should damage the barrel and let the gunpowder spill out. After a while, trying to fight down the terrible fear, he began to work out in his mind what would have happened after he was kidnapped.

Tessa would have made for home. His mother, seeing the pony riderless, would send word to his father who would start a search at once. The search party would look for him along the road and the drive to the mill-owner's house. Colonel Tranton would remember the dogs' uneasiness, the bolting pony he had thought to be a wild one off the moor. Sampson would tell of his fruitless search. What would happen then? Another search through the woods, his father perhaps thinking Stephen had been thrown and lost his way in the mist? And if the dogs had not picked up Jed's scent before, it was not likely they would do so now. There was no hope, Stephen thought, that his father could find him.

That left Sam. He would have gone home when the mist thickened but he would probably go up to The Saddle tomorrow morning, expecting Stephen and his father to be there. When they did not appear, what would Sam do?

Stephen gave up. He was too tired to think any more. Then, just as he was giving way to drowsiness, he remembered something Sam had said about the mine workings, one day last year when they had been rabbiting with Shep. The rabbit had disappeared into a tunnel.

"Shep's not a hope of catching it now," Sam had said. "The old workings are like a set of burrows. Plenty of ways out."

Plenty of ways out.

Stephen's heart beat fast with excitement. He was about to start a wild scramble along the tunnel when the hard edge of the barrel warned him of how dangerous that might be. He lay still and thought carefully. He had no metal objects in his pockets. Only the nails in his boots were likely to cause a spark. If he kept his feet tucked well back . . .

Very carefully, trying not to make the slightest sound, he eased himself backwards until he was beyond the barrel. His heart thumped so loudly he thought it must wake Jed but the snores continued. Stephen pressed on. A trickle of earth fell on him and he paused, faced with a new fear. Suppose the tunnel roof gave way . . .

The trickle stopped. Stephen went on again, feeling the tunnel slope upwards,

the air grow fresher. The blackness ahead gave way to a tiny patch of grey. Another trickle of earth and small stones warned him that he must still be very careful.

At last his head was free of the tunnel and now he was glad of the damp, cool air. For the moment he was out of Jed's reach. But not out of danger. One false move could send him hurtling down a disused shaft or dislodge enough stones to make a clatter which could wake his captor. If only the mist would clear a little . . .

Suddenly, there *was* a break. Only a short one but sufficient to show him he was on the open hillside. Then another momentary break revealed the stunted alder tree Sam had mentioned. On his back, pushing with his feet and arms, Stephen made his way towards the tree.

It was hard work. Tough heather stalks
scratched his face. The gag was hurting
his mouth. But at last he reached the
tree and saw that it grew amongst a
tangle of gorse and bracken, its roots
under a huge boulder. Here he was

completely hidden even if the mist lifted.

Thankfully he leaned back against the boulder. As his bound hands felt the rough granite he had another rush of hope. If he rubbed the rope against the rock, perhaps it would fray. He started too impatiently and skinned his wrist. He tried again, more slowly, rubbing at the rope until it felt quite thin. Then he forced his wrists apart. The rope broke. He was free.

Quickly he untied the gag, then tackled the rope round his ankles, listening anxiously for any sound from the other side of the mine working. When his legs were free he stood up, stiff and sore but triumphant. He saw that the mist was lifting, enough for him to make out a sheep track leading upwards through the heather. He took off his boots so that he could tread more quietly, tied them round his neck and cautiously left his hiding-place. Bent low, he followed the track, not knowing where it would lead him for he had lost all sense of direction and there was no sun to guide him.

Then, abruptly, he was free of the mist, Cuckoo Tor just above him, The Saddle in full view. And standing on The Saddle was Sam.

Stephen opened his mouth to shout

to Sam. Then he realised that if Jed was awake, he would hear him. And Jed, angered by the knowledge that his captive was free, would be very dangerous indeed.

Stephen made his way around the far side of Cuckoo Tor and came up on Sam from behind.

"Whatever's happened to you?" demanded Sam, shocked by Stephen's appearance. "And what's going on down there?"

He pointed to where several men, and the two dogs, were searching amongst bushes near Colonel Tranton's property.

"They're looking for *me*," said Stephen. "Yell, Sam, and wave."

"But what . . . ?"

"I'll tell you later. But we've got to make them see us."

The boys shouted and waved. The men looked up. Stephen thought he heard his father's voice, calling his name. He came suddenly to the end of his strength. His legs gave way and he collapsed in a heap at Sam's feet.

"There's still the barrel of gunpowder, and Jed Upcott," said Stephen's father.

They were in the kitchen, his mother bathing his face and wrists. Sam was there, and Colonel Tranton and Ned Yeo, the foreman. It had been like a birthday party, with cider and cake, his mother laughing and crying at the same time, even Bessie carried downstairs to give Stephen a hug. Now the laughter was over, the men's faces grave.

"Sampson and I will go after Upcott," said the colonel. "A warning shot or two should scare him off. You, boy — Sam, is it — will you lead us to the place?"

"Yes, sir," Sam answered eagerly.

"I'll come, too," said Stephen. Tired though he was, he was not going to miss the excitement.

"Oh, no, you won't," said his

mother, holding him back. "There'll be no more risking of *your* life."

"But don't you see," exclaimed Stephen, furious at being treated like a child in front of Sam and the three men. "Don't you *see*? If I show myself so that Jed knows I'm not still in the tunnel,

75

there'll be no reason for him to set light to the gunpowder."

There was a moment's silence. Then the colonel exclaimed, "The boy's right." He turned to Stephen's mother. "I give my word, Mrs Webber, we won't let any more harm come to your son." He went to the door and called Sampson. "We've a job to do, a surprise attack. The enemy consists of only one man but he's drunk and half-crazed and therefore dangerous. Now then, we'll set off in this order . . . "

Sam whispered to Stephen. "It's a pity we haven't a flag and a drum."

"That would more likely scare Jed than the gun," Stephen said, and then they were both laughing, just as if it was a game.

But when they came within sight of the mine workings, with shreds of mist

again swirling around Cuckoo Tor and
the light beginning to fade, even Sam
looked anxious.

"I think we should stop here, sir," he
said to the colonel. "If you'll all keep
out of sight behind these rocks, I'll take
a look and see if Jed is still there."

He climbed on a boulder and peered through a narrow gap. "Yes, he's there," he called down quietly, "standing beside the tunnel."

The colonel's voice was hoarse with excitement. "Is the fellow near enough to be picked off? If so, Sampson could down him if he shows any sign of firing the powder." He turned to Ned Yeo.

"Help me climb up. I'll see for myself."

But with only one arm it was more than he could manage. He fell on top of the foreman, swearing loudly.

"Jed's heard us," called Sam. "He's looking this way. He's — he's taking matches from his pocket."

"Lie flat, all of you," ordered Stephen's father.

Sam leaped from the rock and sprawled beside Stephen. But Sampson stepped out from the rocks, raised his rifle.

"Lie down, you fool," yelled Tom Webber. "It's too late."

But the colonel, flat on the ground, was still in command. "Take aim, Sampson. *Fire!*"

The shot and the explosion merged into one tremendous, deafening bang. The earth shook. Sampson was knocked

off his feet. The others cowered beneath
the boulders as stones and great clods of
earth, uprooted heather and gorse and
small trees rose high into the air and fell
all about them. The air was filled with
dust and fumes.

The thud and patter of falling debris ceased. For a moment there was an eerie silence. Then from the moor beyond Cuckoo Tor came the bleating of startled sheep, shrill whinnies and the thudding of hooves as the ponies scattered, the harsh cries of crows as they rose from their feeding.

Colonel Tranton got to his feet, looking white and shaken. "Did you — did you get him, Sampson?"

Sampson was dabbing at a gash on his forehead. "Yes, sir, but it was too late, as Mr Webber said. The fuse was already alight. Are you all right, sir?"

"Of course I'm all right. A little shaken, naturally, especially when one realises that blast was meant to destroy my home." He turned to Stephen's father. "I am not too proud a man to admit my mistakes, Mr Webber. Forcing you to employ Upcott was one of them. I shall leave such matters entirely in your hands in future. As for you two boys, be at my house at eleven o'clock tomorrow morning, when you will be suitably rewarded for your prompt and courageous actions."

He marched off down the track, Sampson, shouldering his rifle, a few paces behind.

"You two boys cut along, too," said Stephen's father. "Ned and I will just have a look round, make sure all's safe now."

Stephen and Sam went slowly towards The Saddle. Now the danger was over, the excitement drained away, they were both quiet, walking with heads down.

At last Stephen said, "It was something you said about the mine workings that gave me the chance to escape."

"What was that?" asked Sam in surprise.

"That there were plenty of ways out."

Sam faced his friend. "So I saved your life," he said in his usual cheery voice. "I must remember that and next time that bad-tempered old ram of Father's pins me against a wall, *I'll* call for *your* help."

"*I* only deal with dangerous stuff like gunpowder," Stephen retorted, "not silly old sheep."

Grinning, Sam put up his fists.

Author's Note

Although this story is fictional the remains of the Powder Mills can still be seen alongside the B3212 Exeter to Tavistock road over Dartmoor, between Postbridge and Two Bridges.